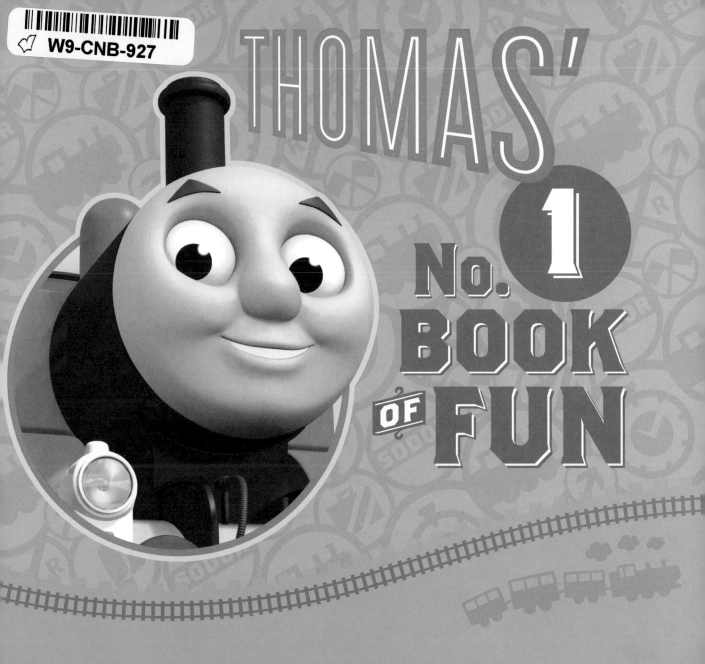

THOMAS'
No. 1
BOOK OF FUN

A GOLDEN BOOK · NEW YORK

Thomas the Tank Engine & Friends ™ CREATED BY BRITT ALLCROFT

Based on the Railway Series by the Reverend W Awdry
© 2017 Gullane (Thomas) LLC.

Thomas the Tank Engine & Friends and Thomas & Friends are trademarks of Gullane (Thomas) Limited.
Thomas the Tank Engine & Friends and Design Is Reg. U.S. Pat. & Tm. Off. © 2017 HIT Entertainment Limited.
All rights reserved. Published in the United States by Golden Books, an imprint of Random House Children's Books, a division of
Penguin Random House LLC, 1745 Broadway, New York, NY 10019, and in Canada by Penguin Random House Canada Limited, Toronto.
Golden Books, A Golden Book, the G colophon, are registered trademarks of Penguin Random House LLC.
Portions of this book were published separately in Great Britain by Egmont UK in the following volumes:
Thomas & Friends Annual 2013, Thomas & Friends Annual 2014,
and Thomas & Friends Annual 2015, in 2011, 2012, and 2013 respectively.

ISBN 978-1-5247-1437-6
www.thomasandfriends.com
randomhousekids.com

MANUFACTURED IN CHINA
10 9 8 7 6 5 4 3 2

Welcome to the Island of Sodor!
Are you ready to be Really Useful— and to have FUN?!

Thomas

NAME: Thomas

COLOR: blue with red boiler bands

SIZE: medium

SPEED: average

PERSONALITY: cheeky, friendly

FEATURES: Thomas has 6 small wheels and a yellow 1 on both his sides.

HISTORY: Thomas started off shunting coaches for bigger engines. Later, he was given his own Branch Line.

Trace
Thomas' name.

Thomas

All About Thomas

Thomas was scared when Cranky lifted him high up into the air.

I look ridiculous!

Thomas was not happy when he was fitted with a silly funnel.

Why do you have a mustache, Sir?

Thomas once mixed up Sir Topham Hatt with his brother, Sir Lowham Hatt!

Color in this picture of Thomas.

Thomas is the Number 1 Engine on Sodor! He always tries his best to be a Really Useful Engine. Everyone loves Thomas — he makes friends wherever he goes!

whistle   dome   funnel

cab window   cab roof   porthole   boiler band   smoke box

coal   boiler body

cab door

side tank

number

chassis side

steps

brake pipe

lamp rod

buffer

coupling hook

counter weight

connecting rod

wheel rim

wheel arch

chassis front

Really Useful Facts

Name: Thomas (You know that!)

Carriages: Annie and Clarabel

Best friend: Percy

Thomas loves: Racing against his friends!

Thomas doesn't like: Being late for a job.

Likes to say: "Peep! Peep!"

Use your crayons to color in this bigger picture of Thomas.
Trace over his name at the bottom of the page, too!

Thomas

★ Meet Percy ★

Percy is a small engine who is full of fun! He is Thomas' best friend and he pulls the mail train. He has lots of accidents too — like crashing into a truck of maple syrup!

Really Useful Facts

Name: Percy

Number: 6

Color: Green

Percy loves: Playing jokes on Gordon and James.

Percy doesn't like: Being called a green caterpillar!

Likes to say: "Mail coming through!"

★ Birthday Time! ★

It's Thomas' birthday! Percy wants to make him a birthday card.

Can you help by drawing a nice picture on the card? You could draw a picture of Percy, some balloons or a birthday cake, or anything you'd like!

Happy Birthday!

James is a very proud engine. He takes tiptop care of his red paintwork. He can sometimes get into trouble for showing off, though!

JAMES **NO5**

No. 5 Red Engine

Really Useful Facts

Name: James

Number: 5

Color: Red

James loves: Pulling the Express when Gordon is away.

James doesn't like: Getting dirty!

Likes to say: "I am a Splendid Engine!"

★ Pink Picture ★

Oh, no! James has been painted pink by mistake!
He's not very happy.

Can you find the **four** objects at the bottom of the page
in the big picture? Check the box when you find one.

a

b

c

d

Thomas' Special Delivery

Help Thomas deliver a new hat to Sir Topham Hatt. But watch out for fallen trees on the track!

★ Shadow Match ★

Draw lines to match Thomas and his friends with their shadows.

 1
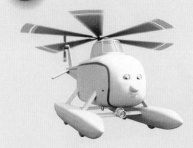

 a

2

b

 3

c

 4

d

Cranky

NAME: Cranky

COLOR: dark green

SIZE: very tall

SPEED: slow

PERSONALITY: grumpy, proud

FEATURES: Cranky has a long, strong crane arm for lifting. He is very tall, so he can see everything that happens at the Docks!

HISTORY: Cranky came to Sodor to help lift heavy loads at Brendam Docks.

Trace Cranky's name.

Cranky

All About Cranky

Get me down!

Cranky sometimes tries to sleep without the engines noticing!

YAWN!

Thomas was stuck in the air when Cranky's crane arm broke!

Oooh, this is hard work!

Lifting heavy loads all day can make Cranky extra grumpy!

Color in this picture of Cranky.

CRANKY

Did you know?

Cranky can be taken apart and moved to other places.

Victor

NAME: Victor

COLOR: red with yellow boiler bands

SIZE: little

SPEED: average

PERSONALITY: wise, friendly

FEATURES: Victor has hazard stripes on his buffer beams and a lamp above his face, to light his way.

HISTORY: Victor came to Sodor to help manage the Steamworks. He also gave Thomas spare parts to help restore Hiro.

Trace
Victor's name.

Victor

All About Victor

Humph! This is just great.

Victor wasn't happy when James blew black soot over him!

ZZZZZZZZ

Victor and Kevin sleep outside the Steamworks after a hard day's work.

Victor sometimes gets cross with Kevin for being clumsy, but they make a good team.

Color in this picture of Victor.

Did you know?

When Victor went away, Thomas was left in charge of the Steamworks. He didn't do a very good job!

★ Creaky Cranky ★

It was an **exciting day** on the Island of Sodor. The Duke and Duchess of Boxford were having a spring party! At Brendam Docks, Cranky was busy unloading cargo for the party, when Thomas chuffed onto the dockside.

"It's the Duke and Duchess' party today!" Thomas said happily.

"I don't go to parties," Cranky grumbled loudly. "I'm stuck here."

"You're *creaky*, Cranky! Is everything too heavy for you?" teased Thomas.

But Cranky wasn't in the mood for jokes. "You couldn't pull anything heavy, *tiny Thomas*! That's why Henry and James have the heavy loads today!" Cranky snapped back.

"I'll prove I'm as **strong** as any other engine!" Thomas told Cranky, and he puffed away to find James. He thought there was more than enough time for him to make his delivery later.

Thomas found James at the Washdown.

"Shall I deliver your wood and barrels to the Docks?" he asked James. "Then you can get ready for the party."

James thought it was a wonderful idea, and soon Thomas was coupled to James' heavy flatbed.

Huffing and puffing, Thomas set off for the Docks.

Thomas **dared** Cranky to try to lift the flatbed. He didn't think the crane would be able to do it. But Cranky did! Thomas was disappointed. He steamed off to find Henry.

Henry was waiting at the coal hopper, so Thomas offered to take his straw bales for him. Henry was delighted.

"Thank you, helpful Thomas!" Henry smiled at him.

Thomas huffed hard to get the straw bales to the Docks, but Cranky managed to lift that flatbed, too. This made Thomas really cross!

"Try lifting *me*, Cranky!" Thomas teased the crane.

Cranky didn't want to let Thomas win, so he lowered his hook. But as he lifted Thomas,

his crane arm stuttered and **snapped**. Thomas was left hanging in the air!

Sir Topham Hatt arrived at the Docks. "You are causing confusion and delay," he told Thomas. "Cranky is broken, and no deliveries have been made!"

Thomas was very sorry. He knew the delays were all his fault. When the Engineer lowered him onto the track, he set about putting things right. He asked **strong** Spencer to take the wood and straw to the party. Then he set off to collect new parts for Cranky from Victor and Kevin at the Steamworks.

Thomas **rushed** back to the Docks with the heavy parts for Cranky. Cranky was really grateful for Thomas' help.

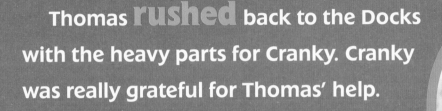

"Thank you, Thomas," Cranky said. "You're not so *tiny*, after all."

"And you're not *creaky* either," laughed Thomas as the friends smiled at each other. Thomas decided not to go to the Duke and Duchess' party. He stayed at the Docks so he and Cranky could have their **own party** instead!

THE END

Gordon

NAME: Gordon

COLOR: blue, with red and yellow lining

SIZE: big

SPEED: fast

PERSONALITY: proud, big-headed

FEATURES: Gordon is the strongest engine on Sodor. He pulls the passenger Express train.

HISTORY: Gordon has pulled the Queen's royal train and visited London. Before he arrived on Sodor, he was painted dark green.

Trace Gordon's name.

Gordon

All About Gordon

Gordon got a shock when a huge snowball rolled down the line!

Brrr, this is going to be chilly!

Gordon came to a sudden stop when a tree fell on the track!

Gordon wasn't happy when Edward was given a more important job than his!

It's just not fair!

Color in this picture of Gordon.

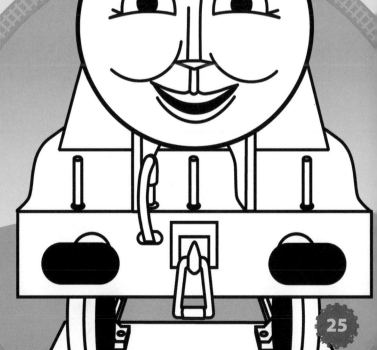

Did you know?

Gordon hates pulling goods trucks so much, he runs into ditches and stops on hills on purpose!

Gordon Runs Dry

Read this story all about Gordon the Big Engine.
When you see a picture, say the word.

 Gordon  Paxton  Thomas

signal water tower

It was a sunny day on Sodor.  was hurrying along

with his trucks of stone. Suddenly the turned red

and 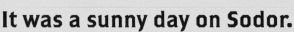 had to stop quickly.  was steaming

the other way. "Express coming through!" he boomed.

But a big stone flew out of the diesel engine's

truck and bashed on his boiler.

 hadn't gone far when his boiler began to run dry.

"That's funny," he said. "I thought I had lots of water."

So he stopped to fill up his tank at a .

 raced off, but soon he had to stop again—his

boiler was almost empty. His Driver filled up the tank with

water, but the passengers were cross. "This is a very slow

train!" they grumbled.

A little farther down the line, was thirsty again.

But this time he whooshed straight past the .

"No time to stop, no time to stop," he worried.

 whirred on, but soon he had no puff left and his

wheels wouldn't turn. "I've run out of steam!" he cried.

Just then, and arrived. "There's a hole

in your boiler, ! You're leaking water," said .

Then remembered the stone. He felt very silly.

He knew that he should have been more careful.

"Don't worry, . I'll take your passengers,"

said kindly.

"Oh, the indignity!" huffed sadly.

But this time he did as he was told. The next day,

pulled into Knapford with his boiler mended. When he

stopped at the , the other engines laughed.

 wasn't pleased, but he knew that Really Useful

Engines look after their boilers, and he was careful never

to run out of water again.

Kevin and Victor Maze

Kevin's late for a job at the Steamworks. Help him get through the maze to Victor as quickly as possible.

Find the Difference

Can you find the 6 differences in the second picture of Thomas and Sir Topham Hatt?

①

②

Answers: Sir Topham Hatt's hat is blue and his pants are green, a squirrel has appeared, Thomas' funnel has disappeared, and his buffer is purple, and Harold has appeared.

♪♪ Sing-Along ♪♪

Join in with this song all about the engines,
then try to answer the questions.

They're 2, they're 4, they're 6, they're 8,
Shunting trucks and hauling freight.
Red and green and brown and blue,
They're the Really Useful crew!

All with different roles to play
Round Tidmouth Sheds or far away.
Down the hills and round the bends,
Thomas and his friends.

Thomas, he's the cheeky one,
James is vain but lots of fun.
Percy pulls the mail on time,
Gordon thunders down the line.
Emily really knows her stuff,
Henry toots and huffs and puffs,
Edward wants to help and share,
Toby, well, let's say he's square!

Sir Topham Hatt's Questions

1. Who thunders down the line?
2. Who is engine number 6?
3. What is the name of the splendid red engine?
4. Where would you find the engine sheds?
5. Which engine looks square?

Come and join in!

Answers: 1) Gordon, 2) Percy, 3) James, 4) Tidmouth, 5) Toby.

33

Hiro

NAME: Hiro

COLOR: black with gold bands and red wheels

SIZE: large

SPEED: average

PERSONALITY: wise, kind, friendly

FEATURES: Hiro has a lamp, his name on a gold plate, and the number 51 on his tender.

HISTORY: Hiro is a very old engine. He was forgotten until Thomas found him and helped to get him restored!

Trace
Hiro's name.

Hiro

All About Hiro!

QUACK! QUACK!

QUACK!

I don't like looking scruffy!

Percy and Hiro like to relax with the ducks by the lake.

When Thomas found Hiro, he was very rusty and dirty. Even his lamp was broken!

Sorry, Sir!

Hiro was red-faced when he made Sir Topham Hatt cross for not being Really Useful.

Color in this picture of Hiro.

Did you know?
Hiro was the first steam engine to arrive on Sodor.

Hiro is a special engine. He was forgotten for many years . . . until Thomas found him again! Now he is a very happy engine!

MASTER of the RAILWAY 51
The Island Of Sodor

Really Useful Facts

Name: Hiro (You know this!)

Color: Black and gold (You know this, too!)

History: Hiro is from Japan.

Fun fact: Hiro's friends call him "The Master of the Railway"!

Hiro loves: Pulling flower trucks.

Hiro doesn't like: Missing home in Japan.

★ My Home ★

Hiro loves to talk about his home in Japan. Now he wants to find out where you live!

Draw a picture of your home. Remember to draw the doors and windows and anything else you want to show Hiro.

Hiro Helps Out

Enjoy this story about Hiro, who helps everyone out!

1 One day, as he puffed into Knapford, Hiro saw that Sir Topham Hatt was missing his hat!

2 He looked very worried. "Oh, dear! What a busy day. Where is my hat?" he said.

3 Edward puffed up. "Sir Topham Hatt is worried about his busy day," Hiro said.

4 Sir Topham Hatt returned with his hat. "I have a meeting about the railway," he said, and quickly left.

5 Edward was worried. "I haven't been told where to take my passengers," he wheeshed.

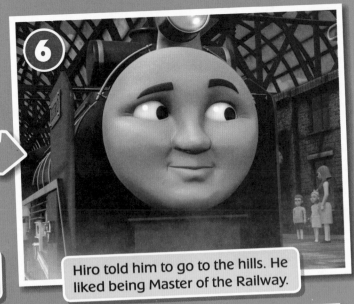

6 Hiro told him to go to the hills. He liked being Master of the Railway.

7 Later, Hiro met Thomas. He was going to ask Sir Topham Hatt where to take his trucks.

8 "Sir Topham Hatt is very busy," said Hiro. "Wait until later." Hiro enjoyed helping Sir Topham Hatt.

QUACK, QUACK!

9 Then Hiro met Percy. He was going to ask Sir Topham Hatt where to take his load of ducks.

10 "Sir Topham Hatt is very busy," Hiro said. "It will have to wait."

11 Then Hiro met Sir Topham Hatt. He was very cross. "None of my engines have done their jobs!" he boomed.

12 Hiro felt terrible. He thought he was helping. "I'm sorry, Sir," he said. "I'll fix this mess right away!"

13 Hiro found Edward in the hills. He sent him to Knapford to see Sir Topham Hatt.

14 He found Thomas by the farm and then wheeshed off to find Percy too.

15 Hiro puffed into Knapford. All the engines had left to do their jobs. "What should I do?" he asked Sir Topham Hatt nervously.

16 "The same as always." Sir Topham Hatt smiled. "You will be Helpful Hiro . . . helping me!" Hiro couldn't have been happier!

THE END

Really Useful Thomas!

Sir Topham Hatt gives a special card to engines who are Really Useful. Thomas has impressed him today, so color in Thomas to complete his card!

REALLY USEFUL

★ Meet Emily ★

Emily is painted emerald green—she really stands out! She can be bossy, but she will always help her friends. She's like a big sister to some of the engines.

EXCELLENT EMILY!

Really Useful Facts

Name: *Emily*

Color: *Emerald green*

Pulls: *Passenger coaches*

Emily loves: *Being right!*

Emily doesn't like: *When the engines won't do as she says.*

Most likely to say: *"Don't call me Little Miss Bossy Buffers!"*

Emily has brought lots of passengers to the fair.
What a Useful Engine!

Find the close-ups in the big picture.
When you find them, check the box and say, "Excellent Emily!"

a

b

c

d

Muddy Matters

Today was the Farmers' Fair. James had
two Very Important jobs to do. He was taking
Farmer McColl's sheep to the fair, and he was having
his photograph taken for the newspaper!

"Make sure you take the fast track to the fair.
No bumping my sheep about," Farmer McColl
had said. "And make sure they stay clean."

"I will keep them as smart as I am, sir!"
James said proudly.

There were two routes to the fair.
One track was fast but muddy. The other track
was bumpy but dry. James didn't want to be dirty
for his photograph, so he took the bumpy track.

The poor sheep **jiggled** about in the back!

"Bubbling boilers!" said James. "What a rocky ride!"

The trailer was bumping so hard, the trailer door
flew open!

But James didn't notice. He was too busy
being the cleanest engine on Sodor.

James pulled up next to Emily at Maron Station. He told her about the photograph for the newspaper. He was so busy showing off, he didn't hear the clack of the trailer. Or the **clatter** of little hooves. . . .

The sheep had escaped!

"**Fenders and fireboxes!**" said James, when he saw a sheep on the platform. "Come back!"

But it was too late. The sheep escaped to the bottom of the field.

The fast train track to the sheep was muddy. So James took the dry track instead. He couldn't get dirty before his photograph!

But the track was very long. By the time James found the sheep, they had already moved away.

"Bother!" said James. Then he had an idea. Katy the sheepdog could round up the sheep. Katy barked, and sure enough the sheep trotted over to James.

"It's working!" said James. "All I have to do is wait here and stay clean!"

James was so excited he let out a whistle. **TOOT!**
But the sheep were so surprised, they ran back into
the field and through a muddy puddle!

"Oh no! We can't be late!" cried James. "It doesn't
matter if I'm dirty. I can't let Farmer McColl down."

So James **whooshed** like the wind down the fast,
dirty track. Soon James wasn't a bright red engine.
He was a muddy, messy one!

James pulled up next to the sheep and
Katy herded them into the trailer. They were
back on track!

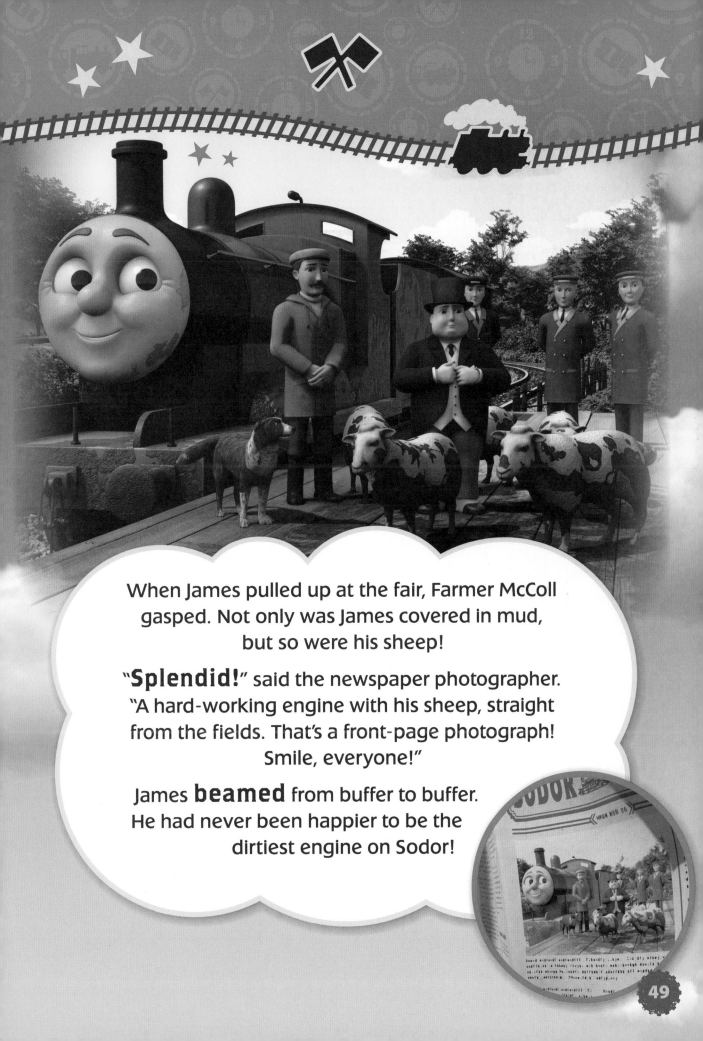

When James pulled up at the fair, Farmer McColl gasped. Not only was James covered in mud, but so were his sheep!

"**Splendid!**" said the newspaper photographer. "A hard-working engine with his sheep, straight from the fields. That's a front-page photograph! Smile, everyone!"

James **beamed** from buffer to buffer. He had never been happier to be the dirtiest engine on Sodor!

☆ Counting Sheep ☆

How many sheep can you count?
Write the number in the box.

I can count ☐ sheep.

☆ Special Deliveries ☆

Thomas and his friends all have special deliveries to make today. Follow the winding tracks to find out what they are delivering.

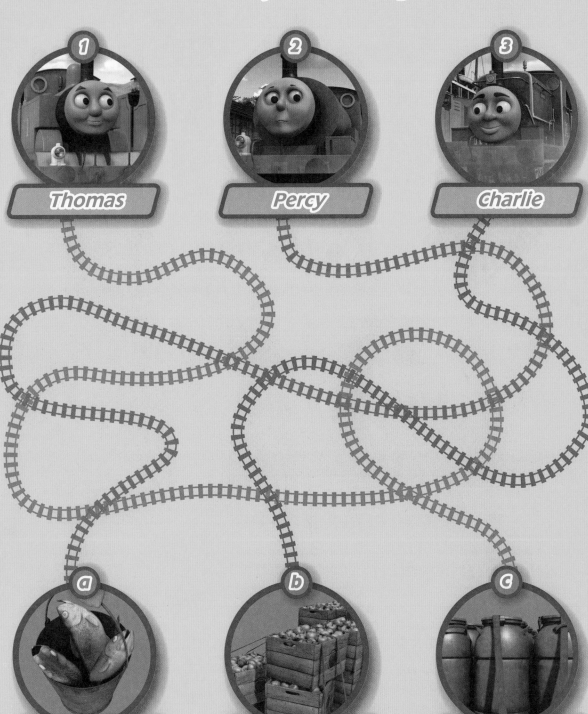

1 Thomas

2 Percy

3 Charlie

a fish

b apples

c milk cans

★ Meet Stephen ★

Stephen is one of the oldest steam engines on Sodor. Although he isn't very fast now, he used to be known as The Rocket years ago!

Really Useful Facts

Name: Stephen

Nickname: The Rocket

Color: Yellow and black

Stephen loves: Helping out at the castle.

Stephen doesn't like: Being left out.

Likes to say: "How can I help?"

☆ Design a Badge ☆

Many years ago, Stephen was given a badge. Now you can make him a new badge!

Grab your brightest crayons and design a badge below. You can draw a picture of Stephen, a castle or anything else you can think of!

You can help read this story. Say the word when you see the picture.

Sodor Railway Royalty

 Thomas

 Stephen

 The Earl

 crown

 and his friends were very excited.

Something special was happening on Sodor.

 was rebuilding the old castle! Percy,

James, and  needed to work as a team to

help him. "Sir, why are we fixing the castle?"

said  . "It's a big surprise," said  .

 had brought his old engine ,

but he had to be repaired first. Victor fixed his

funnel and boiler and gave him a new coat of

paint. "Now you look Really Useful again!"

said .

 wished he could be useful again but didn't know how. "You can be,"  said. " has a top secret job for you!"  steamed off to get started. But he got trapped in an old mine where he found a gold  !

 worked hard to rescue his friend from the mine. was very happy.  had found the gold ! It had been missing for years. "Your special job is to show visitors around the castle,  !" peeped .

 would be a Really Useful Engine again!

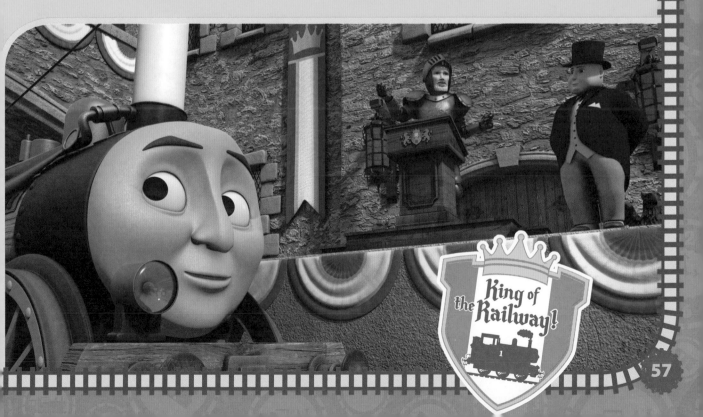

Let's go to . . .

The Animal

How many children can you see in the picture?

Wow! Look at that tall animal. What a long neck it has! I thought I was big, but he makes me feel SMALL!

What's your favorite animal? Draw it here.

58

ark

What colors are the stripes on the wall? Can you think of an animal with the same stripes?

What animal has Thomas delivered to the Animal Park?

giraffe

Gordon got scared when he heard the animals in the Animal Park for the first time!

Answer: There are 5 children in the picture.

Emergency!

Use your finger to help fiery Flynn race through the maze to put out a fire at Ulfstead Castle!

You should pass through five **green** flags along the way.

START

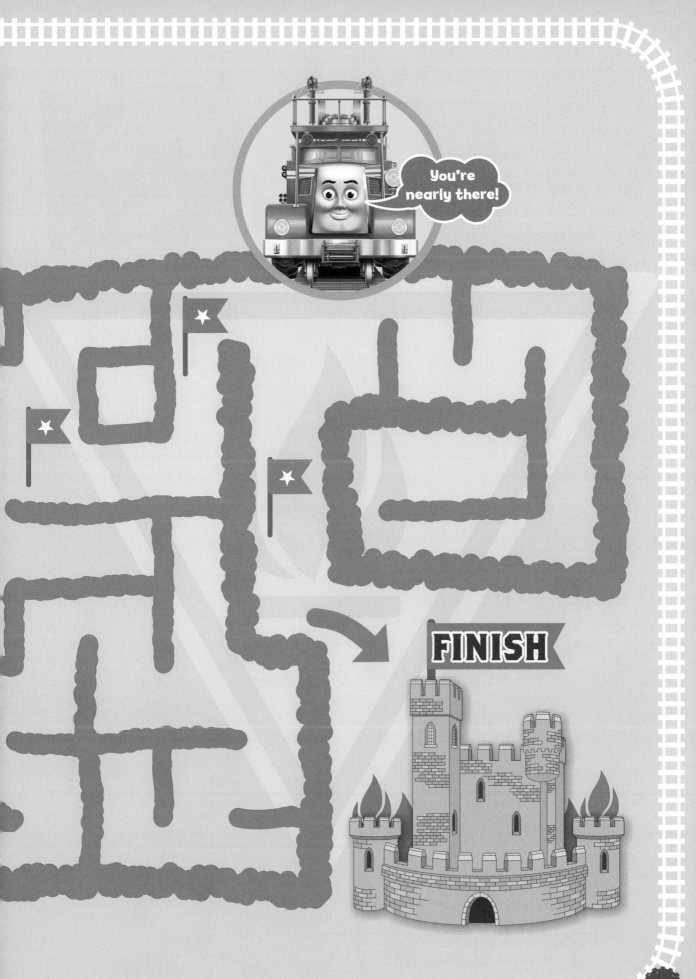

Millie

love, Millie x

Millie is a beautiful blue tank engine who runs on Narrow Gauge rails. Millie lives and works at Ulfstead Castle with her owner, Sir Robert Norramby. Her job is to take visitors on a tour of the Castle in an open-topped carriage!

Best friend: Luke
Fuel: Coal
Paintwork: Blue
Millie loves: Her job pulling passengers around Ulfstead Castle.
Millie doesn't like: Being shut up in her shed.

Sir Topham Hatt's Fact:
Millie comes from France. Instead of saying "hello," Millie says "bonjour" when she sees her friends. Now you say "bonjour."

Splendid!

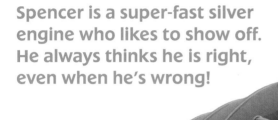

Spencer is a super-fast silver engine who likes to show off. He always thinks he is right, even when he's wrong!

Really Useful Facts

Name: *Spencer*

Color: *Silver*

Fun fact: *He takes the Duke and Duchess of Boxford around Sodor when they visit!*

Spencer doesn't like: *When engines are faster than him!*

Most likely to say: *"Look how fast I am, everyone!"*

The Best Present of All

It was a special day on Sodor. Hiro had come back for a visit.

1

"Let's have a welcome party," said Percy. "Let's get a present," said Thomas.

2

Thomas puffed off to look for a present. He would tell everyone about the party, too.

3

I'm getting Hiro a present!

4 Thomas told Emily he was getting a present. He forgot to invite her to the party!

5 He told Victor about the present, but he forgot to invite him to the party, too!

6 Thomas saw Henry and Gordon, too, but he still only talked about the present!

7 Thomas was chuffing to see Hiro, when he realized. "Oh, no!" he wheeshed. "I haven't told anyone about the party!"

8 Thomas raced around Sodor. He told Emily, Victor, Henry, and Gordon about the party. But then he realized he hadn't gotten a present for Hiro!

9 All the engines were at Hiro's party. Thomas was still sad about not having a present for Hiro.

10 "But you did get me a present." Hiro smiled. "Having all my friends here is the very best present of all!"

THE END

Rattling Rods!

Salty has to get his rattling rods repaired. Which path leads him to Den at the Dieselworks?

At the Engine Sheds

1 How many blue engines are there?

2 Where is Emily?

3 How many green engines are there?

4 Where is Toby?

6 Which engine do you like best?

5 How many engines are there altogether?

Answers: 1. 3; **2.** Emily is the third engine from the right; **3.** 3; **4.** Toby is on the right. **5.** There are 8 engines altogether.

Top Ten Engines

Meet the Sodor engines numbered 1 to 10!

Which **engine or engines** do you like best? Write their numbers here. _____

Percy is **number 6**.
He is best friends with Thomas and he loves pulling the mail train.

James is **number 5**.
He loves pulling coaches but he hates taking Troublesome Trucks!

Toby is **number 7**.
This Steam Tram works on the Quarry Line with his faithful coach, Henrietta.

Duck is **number 8**.
His real name is Montague, but everyone calls him Duck because he waddles on his wheels!

Thomas is **number 1**.
He loves taking passengers
around Sodor in his carriages,
Annie and Clarabel.

Edward is **number 2**.
His Branch Line runs
from Brendam Docks
to Wellsworth Station.

Gordon is **number 4**.
This big Express Engine
is the fastest engine
on the Steam Team.

Henry is **number 3**.
He is proud of his green
paint and he loves going
really fast on the Main Line.

Donald is **number 9**.
He is twins with Douglas.
They came from Scotland
to join the Steam Team.

Douglas is **number 10**.
The twins were numbered
by Sir Topham Hatt when he
decided to keep them both.

Happy Birthday, Sir!

Today was a special day. It was
Sir Topham Hatt's birthday, and there
was a new car on Sodor. He was called
Winston, and he could ride on rails!

"Thomas, take Winston on your jobs today,"
said Sir Topham Hatt. "I'll meet you at
Knapford Station at tea time."

Thomas **beamed** from buffer to buffer.
He was very proud to be helping
Sir Topham Hatt on his birthday!

Salty had a story to tell the engines.

"Many years ago, on his birthday, Sir Topham Hatt visited all the stations on Sodor and had cake with the passengers!"

"Ah, yes, in the oldest carriage on the Island!" said Edward. "Nobody has seen that carriage for years."

"That's nice, Salty," said Thomas. "But we have lots to do. Come on, Winston."

But Winston wasn't thinking about jobs. He was thinking about Sir Topham Hatt's birthday.

The first stop for Thomas and Winston was
Maron Station to pick up some apples.

The workmen coupled up the flatbeds in
no time. Thomas was soon ready to go! But where was
Winston? He wasn't behind Thomas.
In fact, Thomas couldn't see him anywhere.

Suddenly he **burst** out of the bushes!
"Sorry, Thomas! I was looking for . . ."

But there was no time to listen.
Thomas had too much to do!

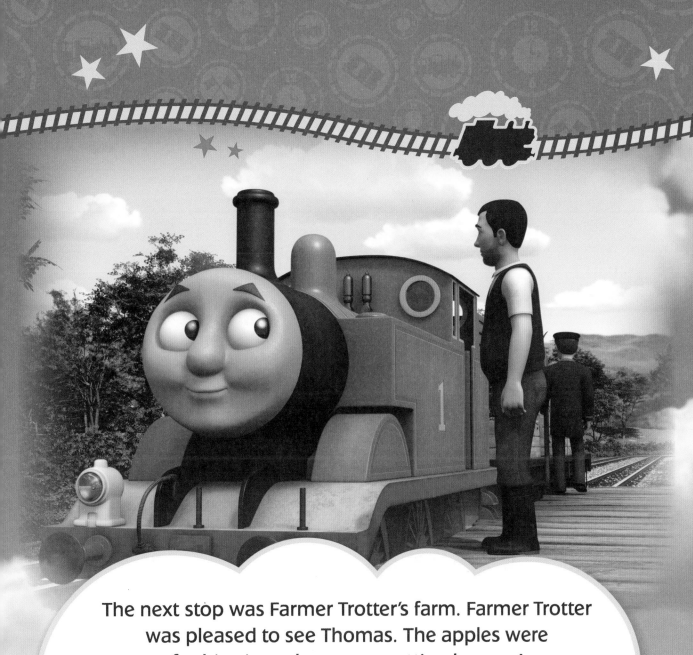

The next stop was Farmer Trotter's farm. Farmer Trotter was pleased to see Thomas. The apples were for his pigs—they were getting hungry!

"See how important it is to be on time, Winston?" asked Thomas. But there was no answer.

Winston had disappeared again! But not for long. He soon **whizzed** back onto the track.

"Sorry, Thomas! I was looking for . . ."

But Thomas was already steaming to the next job!

At the Whispering Wood, Winston vanished again.

"Right, you ride in front of me," said Thomas. "Then I can't lose you!"

Suddenly, Winston came to a stop. "Thomas! That's it!"

There, hidden in the bushes, was Sir Topham Hatt's old carriage!

"That's why you kept disappearing," said Thomas. "**Well done**, Winston! Let's give Sir Topham Hatt the best birthday surprise ever!"

At Knapford Station, Sir Topham Hatt was cross.
Thomas and Winston were late. Just as he was about to
leave, they **raced** into the station.

"**Wait!** We have a surprise for you, Sir!" said Thomas.

Edward **chuffed** up to the platform — pulling the old
carriage behind him!

"**Oh, my!**" gasped Sir Topham Hatt. "Thank you, Thomas.
Thank you, Winston. You have both had
a Really Useful day!"

And that made Thomas and Winston
happier than ever.

★ Birthday Quiz ★

How much do you remember about the "Happy Birthday, Sir!" story? Take the quiz to find out!

Check the boxes when you know the answer. Good luck!

1 Which of these is Winston?

a

b

c

2 What was Winston looking for?

a

b

c

3 Whose birthday was it?

a

b

c

4 What did Thomas take to Farmer Trotter's farm?

a

b

c

5 What color is Winston?

blue

a

green

b

red

c

★ My Present ★

Thomas has brought a present for you, too!
Is it a toy, a pet, or something different?
Draw a picture of it.